A Magical Journey to Nana-Tucket

illustrated by Deb Binnig

by Jean Dapra

three
bean press

With Thanks

I would like to thank Seneca, Julie and Sandy of Three Bean Press for all of the work, suggestions and enthusiasm they have shown me during every step of the journey to *Nana-Tucket*. Thank you to Deb for fitting a six-month commitment into a month and painting a charming picture of my words. A very special thank-you to all the girlfriends who have said to me, "This is so exciting. I am proud of you!" You all know who you are, and there are not enough words to express my appreciation. Thank you to the interesting and fun ladies of CCF Book Group and The Tuesday Reading Club, where we travel the literary world together. A special thank-you and a hug for Jonathan, Jason and Ann, who will always be my babies in my heart. Your pride is a gift! Thank you, Little Ones: Matthew, Natalie and Perrin; You are the stars in Nana's life! — *Jean Dapra*

A Magical Journey to Nana-Tucket
Published by:
Three Bean Press, LLC
P.O. Box 301711
Jamaica Plain, MA 02130
info@threebeanpress.com • www.threebeanpress.com

Publishers Cataloging-in-Publication Data
Dapra, Jean
A Magical Journey to Nana-Tucket / by Jean Dapra.
p. cm.
Summary: Nana-Tucket is a magical island where grandmothers live. Three grandchildren pay a special Christmastime visit to their Nana on the island and learn about how other families celebrate the holiday.
ISBN 978-0-9882212-5-3.
[1. Children—Fiction. 2. Grandmothers—Fiction. 3. Grandchildren—Fiction. 4. Nantucket—Fiction. 5. Christmas—Fiction. 6. Holiday—Fiction.] I. Binnig, Deb, Ill. II. Title.
LCCN 2013950860

Printed in the USA by Lifetouch through Four Colour Print Group, Louisville, Kentucky.

10 9 8 7 6 5 4 3 2 1

To my own grandmothers, Richard's nonas and
every grandmother in the world, especially the
grandmothers of the men and women who serve our country.
— and—
To Richard: You give me Nantucket
again and again. Je t'aime!

— Jean Dapra

To Lee, Kurt and Karlee: I love you
to the sky and beyond the stars.

— Deb Binnig

Far away out on the ocean, there is an island named Nana-Tucket. It is special in every season.

Nana

In springtime, the sun glistens on the ocean waves. Yellow and white daffodils create sunny carpets everywhere. In summer, whales breach off the shore, pink roses climb high and blue hydrangeas bloom in lacy bouquets. Come fall, bright red cranberries float on the bogs, and plump pumpkins grow on vines in fields. Winter arrives with gusts of wind and gray, foggy days, but the seals still come to play, and the island glitters with holiday lights.

Some think Nana-Tucket is magical because so many grandmothers live on the island. These grandmothers all have different names—there's Grandma, Mimi, Granny, Grammy, Nana, Grand-mère, Oma, Abuela, Nonna, Bubbe, YaYa, Babcia, Gogo, Baba, Grootmoeder and Mormor. Some names reflect a family's heritage and some are given by a grandbaby (whether you are three, six, 12 or even 20 years old, in a grandmother's heart, you are always her grandbaby!). Imagine, all of these names mean the same fantastic word: grandmother!

What do you call your grandmother?

Each December, children from all over the world make a fairy-tale journey to Nana-Tucket for some special time with their grandmothers. As their parents prepare for the holidays at home, these lucky children and their grandmothers get in the Christmas spirit on this enchanted island.

Seven-year-old Matthew, his sister, Natalie, age five, and their four-year-old cousin, Perrin, had filled their backpacks and counted the days until their visit to their Nana on Nana-Tucket.

The cousins held hands as they waited on the dock with other happy children for Obadiah, the incredible whale that would take them to the faraway island. Mrs. Red, a rosy-cheeked, red-headed grandmother, came to oversee the journey. She always wore a red dress, a red hat and red boots.

"Children, Obadiah is here!" she sang out.

Suddenly, the great gray whale with a big smile surfaced. Obadiah was Nana-Tucket's treasure—the legendary ferry that transported children to the island. Everyone marveled at the sight of him. A beautiful Nantucket basket with benches, pillows and cuddly blankets sat on Obadiah's back.

The children hugged their parents good-bye, but Perrin held tightly to her mumma's hand. It was her first trip to Nana-Tucket, and she was a little afraid. Matthew comforted her.

"Perrin, you're going to have so much fun, I promise. I am seven," he said proudly. "I will take care of you."

Mrs. Red helped the children climb aboard Obadiah. Everyone waved, and Obadiah spouted water high in the air.

They were on their way to Nana Tucket!

It was chilly on the ocean, but the children snuggled under their blankets, laughing all the way. Obadiah swam smoothly over the water while the children ate red cookies and sipped hot chocolate. Mrs. Red sure knew how to make the journey fun! Before long, Perrin relaxed, and Matthew and Natalie took care of her.

"Nana bakes all kinds of yummy cookies and has a tent in the bedroom full of toys," Natalie said.

"And she loves to read us books," Matthew chimed in.

That got Perrin excited. "You're a good in-charge friend," she told Matthew.

Obadiah swam past the Brant Point lighthouse and docked on Nana-Tucket where a crowd of grandmothers had gathered to greet their grandbabies. Nana stood in the thick of it, her starfish necklace shining in the sun.

Perrin spotted her. "Nana, it's Perrin!"

Nana beamed and waved, and her dog, Jake, wagged his tail, "Hello!" Even the sun was smiling!

Flags flapped in the sea breeze and a band played, just like in a parade. Yet this band was magic: A dog played the trumpet, a cat played the flute and a turtle played a drum. Oddest of all, a mermaid conducted the band with a hydrangea flower.

The children swiftly slid down Obadiah's tail and ran to Nana's outstretched arms.

Soon they were off to Nana's pretty, gray house on Seashell Lane. The white picket fence in front was decorated with thick pine garlands and red ribbons. A wreath with seashells jingled as they opened the door to the cozy scene inside. The children settled in and put their favorite stuffed animals in just the right places.

It was a magical vacation, just as Nana had promised. The first day, Matthew, Natalie and Perrin made ornaments and strung cranberries and popcorn to decorate the tree. They baked sugar cookies shaped like stars, trees and even whales—just like Obadiah. And they built a gingerbread house trimmed to look like Nana's house.

"May we take some cookies for Mrs. Red, as a surprise, when we go home?" Perrin wanted to know.

"What a nice thought," Nana replied. "Of course you may."

The children sang Christmas carols and ate cookies with Nana, laughed and ate cookies, read stories and ate cookies, and gave hugs and ate even more cookies! Jake, the dog, ate a cookie, too.

"Can we have cookies for breakfast, please?" the children pleaded.

"Yes, for a special treat," answered Nana. "But you have to eat an orange and drink some milk, because that is a healthy breakfast."

Of course, there were some rules at Nana's. You had to be respectful and have good manners, like saying please and thank you and not burping at the table. But the number one rule was: BE NICE!

Did you ever notice that when you are being good and nice, you are happy?

"Let's learn how other people celebrate Christmas," Nana said, taking the children to visit other grandmothers' homes. "Families have different holiday traditions, from the food they eat to the games they play."

"Feliz Navidad," Abuela greeted. She was from Mexico. At her home, they ate tamales with chicken, raisins and cinnamon with Michael and Gala.

Nonna was Italian, so she taught the kids to play bocce with Anthony and Maria and served slurpy spaghetti and sweet panettone—yum! *"Buon Natale,"* Nonna said, dishing out seconds.

At Grand-mère's, Gabrielle and Jean served a beautiful Yule log cake, a Christmas custom in France (it did not taste at all like wood or twigs!). *"Joyeux Noël,"* Grand-mère said.

One thing was certain—no matter whose home you visited, you could feel the love and joy of family.

On their last full day on the island, Nana said, "I have a special surprise for you tonight."

After dinner, the children bundled up in the new scarves and mittens Nana had knit for them and headed into town holding hands.

Christmas trees brimming with colorful ornaments lined the sidewalks, and shopkeepers passed out treats from stores bedecked in garlands and lights. Nana carried her Nantucket basket purse, and Natalie noticed that all of the other grandmothers had them, too. A man ringing a bell drew attention to carolers who sang familiar Christmas songs and were dressed in old-fashioned clothing.

Then a parade, led by the magic band, marched up the cobblestone street past The Lion's Paw, where Natalie and Perrin found gifts for their mothers, and The Hub, where Matthew bought Swedish fish and postcards. It filed past Mitchell's Book Corner, where the children had picked out books after story time. They found a spot to watch the scene by Nantucket Looms, where Nana loved to buy soft, woolly throws and handmade gifts. When the parade paused at Murray's Toggery Shop, Matthew noticed the popular red pants in the storefront window.

"Those are called 'Nantucket Reds,'" Nana said. "You can only get the real ones at Murray's."

"So, they are special, fancy pants," Matthew laughed. "I like them!"

Nana smiled, tucking the idea away for a future Christmas, and suggested, "Let's walk down by the dock to see how the dory is decorated."

They were all looking at the dory when…all of a sudden, the bell ringer shouted,
"He is here!"

At that very moment, snowflakes fell softly on Nana-Tucket. Silver stars filled the sky and the silver moon smiled. Obadiah swam up to the dock with a splash. And guess who was in the basket on Obadiah's back? SANTA CLAUS!

"Yay, Yay, Hey, Hey," the crowd cheered as Santa stepped onto the dock with an enormous sack of presents. Every gift was the same size, wrapped in red paper with stars and hearts and green ribbon.

The children's faces lit up like lights on a tree. Grand-mère beamed at Gabrielle and Jean; Nonna draped her arms around Maria and Anthony; and Abuela gave Michael and Gala an extra squeeze. Nana bent down close to the children.

"You are the greatest gift I've ever received," she told them.

"Will I receive a present?" Matthew was curious. "I've tried to be a good boy all year."

Natalie answered quickly, "Yes, Matt. And I was good, too."

"Does Santa count time-outs?" Perrin was concerned. "And does he see when you share your favorite toys and use manners and don't fuss?"

Nana explained, "Tonight Santa is delivering a special present to every child here on Nana-Tucket. It is something that cannot be bought or made."

"Will there be trucks, blocks and games?" asked Matthew.

"Santa will leave presents like those at your homes on Christmas Eve," Nana reassured. "These presents are different because they contain all of your grandmother's love, packaged up to carry in your hearts forever."

"How does love get wrapped up?" Natalie wanted to know.

"In each box is a beautiful heart inscribed with fancy gold letters," Nana explained. "No matter how grown up you are, you can always remember its message."

"What does the message say?" Perrin asked.

"It reads, *You are so special, Little One. You are such a good little person. I love you forever and ever and always.*" Nana said, adding, "Each one has the child's grandmother's name on it."

You are so special, Little One.
You are such a good little person.
I love you forever and
ever and always!
Hugs,
Nana

"Are you sure Santa is going to leave other gifts, too?" Matthew asked. "Because I would really like a new football."

"And a ballerina doll and a necklace," Natalie echoed.

"And some hair bows, a baby doll and books!" Perrin exclaimed.

Nana smiled to herself, and she assured the children that Santa would bring those sorts of gifts to their homes on Christmas.

At the top of Main Street, Santa called every child by name. He offered them a candy cane, asked what they wanted for Christmas and handed them one of the special presents.

Back at Nana's, the children carefully opened their gifts.

"These hearts are beautiful!" Natalie said, wide-eyed. "Can we keep them?"

"Of course," Nana answered.

"I'll love it forever!" Perrin said.

Matthew agreed, "It is even better than a toy because it will always make us feel close to you."

They snuggled in special beds by the twinkling Christmas tree that night and dreamed of mermaids, whales, friends, cookies and the grandmothers they met and the hugs they could still feel. They were so happy, and Nana was even happier.

Tucking them in, she kissed each child on the forehead, repeating, "You are so special, Little One. You are such a good little person. I love you forever and ever and always."

The next morning, it was time for the children to return home. Matthew, Natalie and Perrin climbed aboard Obadiah with their belongings and memories, the magic note etched on their hearts and so, so many cookies.

Nana squeezed a penny into the palm of each child's hand. "Toss it in the water as you pass the lighthouse," she told them, "and you will return to Nana-Tucket next year."

Then Obadiah set off with a lurch.

Back on the dock, the grandmothers waved, throwing kisses.

They had received the best present in the world—their grandbabies!